This book belongs to

Tina Harper

CLASS 7.

Cinderella

RETOLD BY

Samantha Easton

ILLUSTRATED BY

Lynn Bywaters

TED SMART

A TED SMART Publication 1995

First published in the USA in 1992 by Andrews and McMeel

ISBN 0 7529 0107 9

Design: Susan Hood and Mike Hortens
Art Direction: Armand Eisen, Mike Hortens and Julie Phillips
Art Production: Lynn Wine
Production: Julie Miller and Lisa Shadid

Cinderella

Once upon a time there lived a rich man whose wife had died. After a time, he married again. His second wife was very proud and ill-tempered, and she had two daughters who were just like her.

Now, this man had a daughter from his first marriage. She was very good and beautiful, which made her stepmother and stepsisters jealous.

It wasn't long before the stepmother and her daughters began to treat the poor girl very badly. They made her do the cooking and cleaning, and gave her only an old grey smock to wear. Instead of sleeping in a bed, she had to sleep on the hearth among the cinders. And that was how she came to be called Cinderella.

One day, Cinderella's stepsisters received invitations to a ball that the king was giving for his son. All the young ladies of the kingdom were invited, for the prince wished to choose one of them as his bride.

Cinderella's stepsisters were overjoyed. From that moment on, they could talk of nothing except what they would wear to the ball.

"I shall wear my gold embroidered gown," said the elder. "The prince will surely notice me in that!"

"And I shall wear my green velvet gown," said the younger. "Mother has always told me I look best in green!"

And on and on they talked and planned. They were each determined to be the most beautiful lady at the ball.

At last, the day arrived.

All day Cinderella's stepsisters shouted orders at her. "Cinderella, iron my silk petticoat!" said one. "Curl my hair!" said the other. "Tie this ribbon!" said the first. "Polish my shoes!" said the other. Cinderella didn't complain but did their every bidding.

At last her stepsisters were dressed and ready. As she saw them to the door, Cinderella could not help but sigh, "How I wish I were going to the ball."

Her stepsisters stared at her. "You?" mocked the elder. "What an idea. How could you go to the ball?"

"Besides, whatever would you wear?" said the younger. "Your tattered grey dress with your patched apron?"

Then they both burst into laughter and stepped into their coach.

After her stepsisters had gone, Cinderella sat by the hearth and cried.

Then a voice beside her asked, "Cinderella, why are you crying?"

Cinderella looked up. There stood a woman wearing a white dress covered with gold stars. In her hand she held a sparkling wand. "I am crying because . . ." she stammered.

"Because you would like to go to the ball," the woman finished for her. "And so you shall. I am your fairy godmother and I have come here tonight to make all your wishes come true."

Before Cinderella could say another word, her fairy godmother led her into the pumpkin patch in the garden. "First, we must choose a large, round pumpkin," she said. "That one looks about right!"

As Cinderella watched in amazement, her fairy godmother waved her magic wand over the pumpkin and it was transformed into a gold coach!

"Now," said Cinderella's fairy godmother, "let us find the mousetrap and see if there are any mice."

Inside the trap were six grey mice. The fairy godmother waved her magic wand again, and in the twinkling of an eye, they were turned into six fine dappled horses.

"Now, let's look in the rattrap," said the fairy godmother. Inside there was a fat white rat. The fairy godmother touched it with her wand, and instead there stood a jolly coachman with wonderful long whiskers.

"Now, go to the lily pond," Cinderella's fairy godmother told her. "If you find six green frogs sitting on a log, bring them to me."

And Cinderella did so. With a wave of her magic wand, her fairy godmother turned the frogs into six merry footmen, all dressed in handsome suits of green.

Cinderella was overjoyed. But then she looked down at her old grey smock and her face fell.

"Don't worry!" her fairy godmother said
kindly. "I have thought of that, too."

She waved her magic wand once more,
and the tattered grey smock became the
most beautiful gown Cinderella had ever
seen. The dress was made of silver and gold,
and was studded with precious gems. Then
her fairy godmother brought from her
pocket a pair of sparkling glass slippers.

"Now, you are ready to go to the ball,"
she said with a smile. "But be warned! You
must return before the clock strikes twelve.
At that hour my magic will fade. Your gold
coach will turn back into a pumpkin. Your
horses will be mice, your coachman, a rat,
and your footmen, only frogs. And your
beautiful gown will once again be a tattered
grey smock."

Cinderella gave her promise. Then she
thanked her fairy godmother and set off
happily to the king's palace.

When Cinderella entered the king's great ballroom, she looked so lovely that everyone stopped talking and eating to look at her.

"Who can she be?" they whispered. Her stepsisters, who did not recognize her, said that Cinderella must be a princess from a faraway land. "Who else would be wearing such a splendid gown?" they murmured.

The prince had never seen such a beautiful lady. Immediately, he introduced himself to her and asked her to dance.

Cinderella smiled and nodded. She danced so gracefully that everyone stopped dancing and watched her in admiration.

All night long the prince danced with Cinderella, and Cinderella only. She had never been so happy. She felt as if she were in a beautiful dream.

Cinderella was enjoying herself so much that she did not notice the time passing. Suddenly, the clock began to strike twelve.

"Good-bye!" she called to the startled prince as she dashed from the ballroom. The prince ran after her, but Cinderella was too quick for him.

In her haste, she lost one of her sparkling glass slippers on the palace steps. But there was no time to stop for anything. Just as she reached the gate, the last stroke of midnight rang out. Her beautiful gown turned back into her old grey smock, and her gold coach coach became a pumpkin. She watched as the mice and the frogs and the rat scurried off. And then she slowly walked home.

The next morning, the prince found Cinderella's glass slipper on the palace steps. It was the most delicate slipper he had ever seen. He carefully picked it up and carried it to his father. "I will marry only the woman whose foot this slipper fits, and no other," he told the king.

At once the king sent his servants throughout the kingdom to try the glass slipper on each lady.

All sorts of young ladies—tall and short, plump and thin, rich and poor—tried on the beautiful glass slipper. But not one of them could get it to fit.

At last, the king's servants came to Cinderella's house. Her two stepsisters were eager to try on the slipper, since they both considered their feet to be small and dainty.

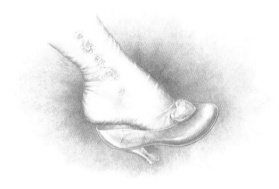

First the elder stepsister tried to get the slipper on, but it would not even go over her toes. She pushed and pulled, but it was no use. Then the younger stepsister tried it on. She tugged and winced, but she could not get the slipper on over her heel.

Then Cinderella said, "May I try, too?"

Her stepsisters rolled their eyes and said, "The slipper will never fit you!"

But the king's servant said that it was only right that she be allowed to try. So Cinderella stretched out her foot.

The stepsisters were surprised. The glass slipper fit Cinderella's foot so perfectly it might just as well have been made for her!

To their further amazement, Cinderella reached into her pocket and brought out the matching glass slipper.

At that moment, Cinderella's fairy godmother appeared, but only Cinderella could see her. With a wave of her magic wand, she turned Cinderella's rags into a gown even more beautiful than the one she had worn to the ball.

Her stepsisters then recognized Cinderella as the lovely princess from the ball. They knelt before her and apologized for treating her so badly. Then Cinderella, who was as kind as she was beautiful, said, "It's all right, sisters. I forgive you both."

The king's servants took Cinderella to the palace to see the prince. He was overjoyed to see her again, and asked her to become his dear wife.

Cinderella and her prince were married that very day. Everyone in the kingdom was invited, even Cinderella's stepmother and stepsisters. It was the most splendid and joyful wedding anyone had ever seen, and Cinderella and her prince lived happily ever after.